SHYROTICA

Let your imagination runs through your vein and submerged in what so-called, the food of body and soul, erotica

Shy Lhen Esposo

Copyright © 2021 SHYROTICA
by Shy Lhen Esposo

This is a work of fiction. Any resemblance to actual persons, living or dead, or actual events is purely coincidental.

Published by Poetry Planet Book Publishing House
Designed and arranged by Tess Ritumalta
Edited by Marie Ezekiel
Preface by the Publisher

Please submit all reviews and comments or report errors to xanderlen.xelaen@gmail.com.

Illustrations used courtesy of Pinterest and Pixabay and may contain its own copywrites.

DEDICATION:

Learn to play your own special game! Beyond anxiety and odds, beyond shyness to boldness beyond difficulties and easiness beyond tears and laughs I have always managed to balance my life I was once, zero knowledge in this world of art in writing, and never had any experience in the past. But, dreams never stop chasing my silent night so here I am, creating once again "SHYROTICA", is my first erotica writing where I found myself sometimes daydreaming, and illusioning that these naughty moves and words could happen and excess in reality and keep it sacredly. Of course, I want this to happen one day with my fate Yes nothing but my fate no one else but my fate.

INTRODUCTION

SHYROTICA is Shy Lhen Esposo's wildest dreams and wet imageries of her indescribable feelings. And most of it is her undying love and passion for writing. Poetry is Shy Lhen Esposo's escape-goat of loneliness and stress reliever, Shy Lhen Esposo never stops believing that all her dreams will come true and will never fail. While reading this book, imagine how she dealt with her Facebook bashers every day, imagine how her imagination lingers on. SHYROTICA", is lustrous, and tempting that you'll never regret what you have read about.

Shyrotica book is her 4th collection published book.

PREFACE

SHYROTICA is not simply just a compilation of erotic poems and short stories. It is a masterpiece to a lover of art. It's fanciful and imaginary, words are seducing, tempting and enticing that can even betray oneself. The book speaks about romance and art of love-making to both masculinity and femininity.

The author's wildest imagination is a product of her astounding literary interest. It's a chimera of words, a fantasy... so quixotic and wild.

The nude paintings of the famous Pablo Picasso viewed by billions in the Museums of Art is always be remembered. For art lovers, they view nudity in painting as a form of masterpiece… For writers and book worms, erotic writing is a product of great scribbling. Both painting and writing are talents that can create works of genius beyond expectation even if some may find it scandalous, but an art is an art, whatever the figure is.

Only the gifted like Shy Lhen Espeso can create a book like "Shyrotica".

Deem with her thoughts. Device what best you can. Dance the rhythm of sex. It's fulfilling and enchanting.

TABLE OF CONTENTS

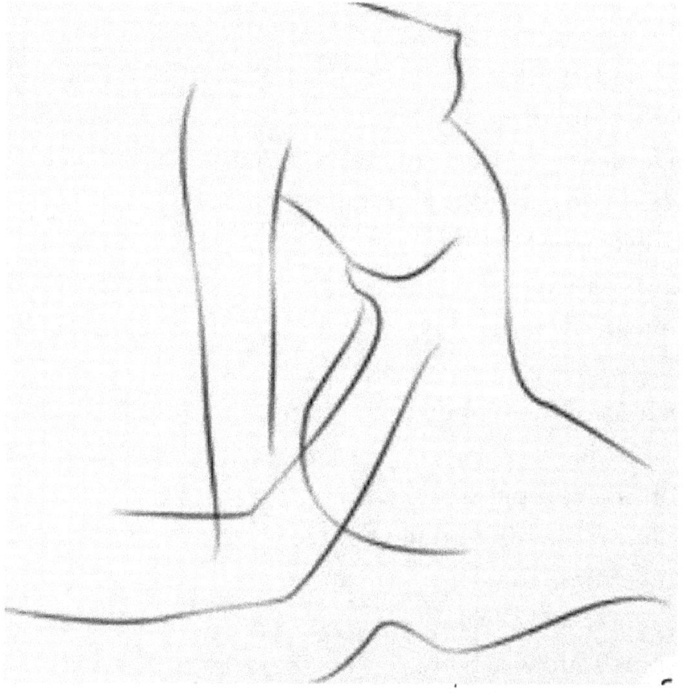

LONELY SHEETS

I pine when you're gone too long.
Clara said,
The bed's too big without you.
My head knows,
but body bulks
mule stubborn
that pleasure, don't run deep enough
when you can't dip with me.
Breasts un-caressed,
tend to them,
hips grind nothing but
lonely sheets.
Jealous of the woods
you love,
nothing competes
to lying-in with you next to me.
Blues come to visit,
I greet my old friend,
but he's lifeless, baby.
Pleasing myself is fun, smoothing hips,
dipping fingers into my well,
I'm just touching what hasn't been mine
for so long.
Pillows shift wrong,
sheets too rough,
sunshine ain't as bright
as it shines.

I need that door knocked now,
sweet rubs,
hugs stealing breath,
love.
waitin's feverish
'til you come home,
voice waking to
 "Baby."
 As you bend down,
some inside shine,
glows again.
You kiss me,
where you miss
me most.

A KISS OF UNDYING AFFAIR

a luscious lust that burns thy souls
fire from the eternal flame
a desire of unfading passions
a kiss that ignites intimate erotica
affection
tongue to tongue, lips to lips
the invading romance of hearts that
may never be together forever
for they are both sinners of thy own
partners
Lovers in the corner.

YOUR ILLUSIONS

The eager you want to have
the love that makes you fly
without wings,
the merrier you long to satisfy
your inner desire of having
lustrous reactions
a simple move that makes your vein
erected by pepping a simple
position that gives you
an urge to lust and cum
without hot sexualization
sit, and take a look at it.

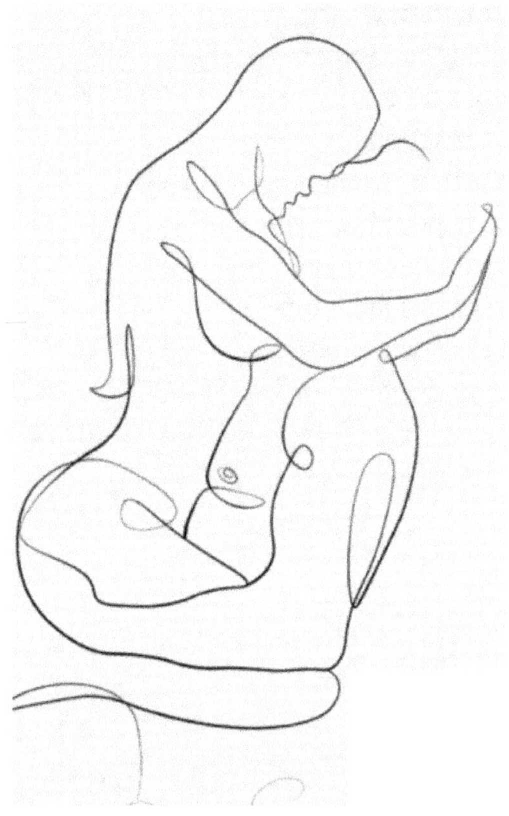

I'M YOURS,

Throughout the busy day
with your busy hours,
I preferred to take a shower
when you reached home,
before I served your dinner,
I loved to give you pleasure
to ease your stressful mind
I knew you need my gentle touch
my sweet caress and hugs
To be as one before everything
around us, was a thing that
satisfied our souls and lusts
felt the love that only for you to have
Held me like you never did before
aroused me with your throbbing vein
Am yours that day, before and after.

SHE'S A WOMAN

She's a woman who lives alone
in this lonely world
searching for a lovely soul who will carry her
from the top of the hill
from there, his reward is her naked soul.
As if he asks a gorgeous breast,
as a price then, here it is all his,
oh, Knight wraps around her arms to her ass
and gently caresses her nakedness
let his tongue teases her tits
while his fingers down to her clit.
Suck em!

SEDUCE...(ACROSTIC /KU'RYU)

S-ensual touch, teasing lips

E-rotically coitusing hard

D-esirable, cummings

U-ltimate lovemaking

C-aressing hands, grasping moans response

E-xploited lovers lust.

IN MY SLEEPLESS NIGHT

I am living in this world that full of imagination
and my unforgettable memory is when I am with
you all alone,
along with those beautiful roses in my bedroom.
While sitting next to you, I love to steal a kiss from
you and, when you turn your head next to my
head, ohhh!!! that flirty smile, seducing my body.
And I can't help to hug you tight, and drag you
closer to my chest and feel my trembling heart.
Your fingers begin to hunt those pinky buds. You
are moving passionately,
you make me sigh, and gasp some more, with your
sweet kisses between my legs. I am burning inside
while, your tongues licking my naked wound,
arousing my skin with your gentle touch, your
sweet nectar that I missed. Those sound with
Satisfaction your hmmm.. ohhh!!! Baby, I want you
in my bed once again and feel the love, the
romantic moment mostly when you're deep inside
of me, moving gently within, between my heart
and memory. You're killing me softly, with
toughness reaching the bottom to the top of my
happiness, My soul is hungry with your love I
can't help my feeling I want you deeper than my
thoughts

Aahhh!!! ohhhhmmm... honey, please don't stop!
please, l want you deeper, harder, and let us cum
together...

 In my sleepless night, all alone
in this empty room imagining you're right here,
where we used to meet, make the world colorful
with our sweats starving souls. You are in my
dreams occupying my emptiness arousing my
nakedness healing my open wound with your
ironic humble dick.
I want to lay down beside you
and let your arms wrap my nakedness
feel your warm body around me.
I want to hold and embrace you tight
I want to hug everything on you
I want to kiss you, from head to toe...
Be with me tonight right next to me
watch me over, while I'm sleeping sweetheart
don't leave me alone for I'll be lonely in the middle
of the night...
Ohh baby, how l missed these fancy moments
being alone with you all night long
been waiting for this, hungry for your touch.
Be my soul's food the whole night and feel the love
l have for you,
for you to cherish and emblem my heart and mine.
For I still remembered the first night we've been
together

your eyes gaze like a flaming fire
your whispers and gasped that burns my soul
your gentle touch and sweet kisses throughout my
nakedness...

Your moaned penetrated my lust
you've shared a priceless desire
that night, when our body became one...

You excite me, baby, come closer and one more
time, let us feel the love tonight
let us feed our souls fill up our thrust
within our gentle touch our sweet caress

Fill up our luscious, savage touch
feel you deeper than the ocean
moan and moan through undying intimate passion.

As we found ourselves as one,
I want you by my side now and forever
I love you, I'll be yours forever Through

TEASERS TEASE

You and me
all alone
holding hands
all the way.

Touching me
touching you
hugging me
hugging you.

Cheek to cheek
eye to eye
lips to lips
sighing deep.

Pulling up
pushing down
moan to moan
gasp to gasp.

Heart and soul
qwerty punch
fingers in
fingers out.

Witty cunt
throbbing vein

wanting us
cum again.

Hardened vein
aroused clit
ohhhs! and. ahhhh...
sultry lust.

Satisfied
beyond lust
against odds
sacred hearts.

ROMANCE

Intimate and passionate
lubricant masterpiece
fantasies of lovers
desirable caress

A mankind habitat
passion of love
satisfaction of souls
momentum of romance

Arisen the beauty of
abstract
Exhibit of hungry
hearts...
Elusive sensational
moves...
arousing touch of
masculine mold...

The art of two hearts
their moves of satisfactions
the titillating reactions
of fulfilling sacred hearts and passions.

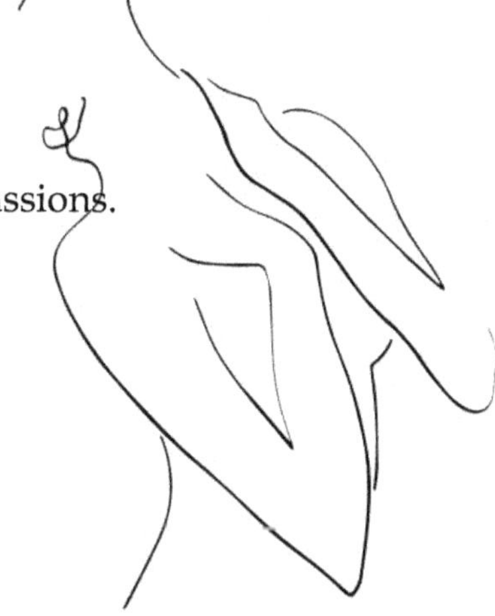

SATISFACTION

A night of fulfilling dreams
a passionate moment
abstract of soulless souls
stroking, brushing ups and down
swaying, feeling each in every silhouette
delivering desirable journey through final
destination.
a lust that lasts like eternal flames
covered with alluring moans
the flirty actions of greedy mankind
until satisfaction is laid.

LOST CONTROL

In the midst of nowhere
we found a place to share
love with the exotic play
naughtiness exists without prey.

As we dance in the rhythm of salsa
he sat and I move dancing cha cha
vogue, shake rolling like marble
on top of a throbbing muscle.

And many times, we lost control
sweet whispers and moan as we stroll
caressing moves through our naked soul

The rhythm of a falling lust
satisfaction satisfied at last
dancing with the sexiest form of romance
titillating, flirty moves subside at once.

AN INTIMATE PASSION

Surfing around my nakedness
moaning like a kitten in my ears
fingers run through my flimsy skin
finding a cave yard underneath my toe
Ohhh!! a feeling of satisfaction
a heart that beats under my shirt
a hard vein entering deep in my womb
deeper as deep within
A sigh that satisfies my lust and the hungry soul
a moan that gives me an intimate passion
a greedy soul that collides, again and again
until we reach the bottom of erotical action

NAUGHTY MOVES

Erotically moves in passion
vividly man's creation
the fatal sensation of
oral demonstration.
The beauty beyond walls
moaning so wild and free
flirty titillation underneath;
abstract of hungry souls
Seducing each part
licking every single piece
arousing, grasping feeling
get through it I'm begging.
Those whispers ohhh.your
gentle touch
arousing moves,
titillating feeling
moaning like dying
dying through intimate passion
sensual sensation
the satisfaction of hungry,
greedy soul
Submissive. Ohhh!!!
lust flirting fingers
runs through a
hungry cave
lust of hungry dick
rubbing through,

hmmm private dancer
dancing in the rhythm
of erotica moves.
Ohhh erecting vein
cum to my wetty cave
Don't stop pumping
go deeper, harder, and faster
let us cum together
stranger soul, I love the
way you love me
don't stop,
Let's dance to the rhythm
of love and lust together
we cum.

PAINFUL, HAPPINESS

You've given me such joy
the feeling of having a favorite toy
in a day of forbidden oneness
you were there, patched my sadness.

As the music goes soft and mellow
you clinched your arms in my waist
as our souls reunited with passion
we want more than a consolation.

We didn't notice we're in the climax
the climax of forbidden love and romance
which we have been having more or so
yet the excitement was always there for you.

Ahhh! four letters as I always whispering
within your ears when start fires flaming
burning my soul so hot and seducing
an intimate passion desirable, igniting.

As we go further than we thought
you've come to find out the meaning of love
ohhh four letters as I whispered to your heart
you gave all the best things ever on my part.

I felt the hardest part of yours inside me,
as you go along with your greedy-manly

I felt the hardest part of yours inside me
whenever you went up and down hard and depth

I felt the pain within happiness
that you let me know how great it was
grasping was the only thing I could do
when you pimped up and down and go.

Sweat sweating sweaty and witty
I called my lord for what have you been to
the wonderful day when our time consumed
with something titillating feeling of lust.

MY AMOR

You were there once again
In my sleepless night like a thief that sneaked
you've stolen my lonely aching heart.
You heard my whisper in the dark
you came across the line of duty
I heard your whistle and husky voice
humming, until you have reached the end of the
road.
I was standing in front of the patio hall
where I can see you walking towards the door
and curtains covered up my nakedness
your perfume fragrance aroused my soul
Your masculine body, your poise, your shadow,
captured my blurring sight and my ambitious
desire lingered
and you were not just a dream to recall
you were here, standing right next to me my Amor
You teased my long blonde hair
streaming, like a guitar on the wall
and your fingers slept in my ears, down to my face
and feel the softness of my lips...
I was frozen of what you were doing
A while ago, I let you feel what I've dreamed of
a savage kiss is what you offered and sailed it away
And I wanted more than your kisses
You're on my bed
My illusions come along

my lonely night becomes the loveliest after all
you and I created the nest of lustrous romance
as you placed your throbbing vein between my legs
and love matters till the end

Woke up in the middle of the night
with your tender kisses and touch.
grasping moaning
that's all you've heard
Your tongue,
that played around my chest
while licking my pinkish tits
your fingers, that tickling
my milky skin.
And held your buttocks tight
when you coitus and went deep into my cunt
humping in so hard
your throbbing dick's perfectly gliding
in and out between my legs
I love the way you aroused me

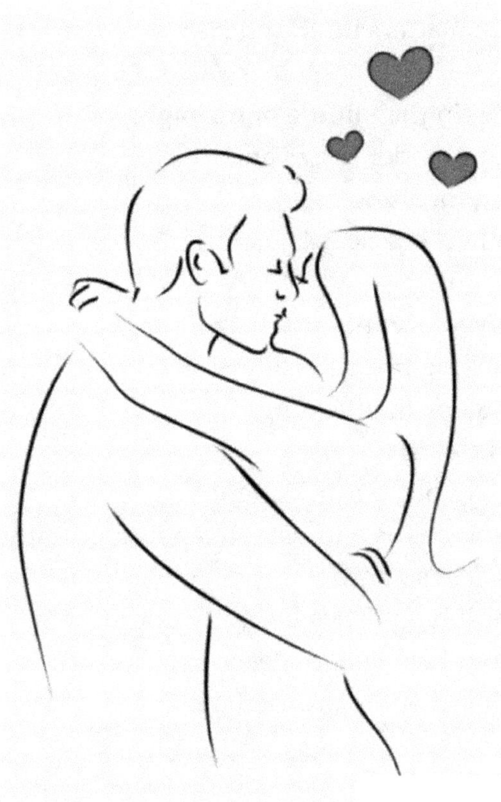

YOUR LUSCIOUS LIPS

Sitting in your lap.
humping, while you coitus
deep and hard
You laid me down,
in the edge of the bed
you split my legs,
You knelt and
started to lick my clit.
savage kiss of
your luscious lips,
your tongue that
teases my witty cave
to moan and grasps
that's all I wanted
I squirted to your mouth
as you wanted to
taste and drink
my ink that dripped
and I did, I cum
through your mouth
as what you desired
and swallowed all my semen.

QUIESCENT

Aftermath.
So good, so sweet, so mine!
Exhaustion born of passion,
we lay curled,
basking at what we have done.
Musk shared replete,
awash in us.
My peanut butter thighs
shift restlessly,
amazingly wanting more.
I sense your movement and realize
that you are still hungry, too.
Furious, we laze now.
You touch me so delicately,
carefully,... yet determined.
I meet you with a kiss,
my body gives a green light,
and lover, you move!
Your big hands, rough fingers, gentle me,
but mutely demands more.
Sheets damp, we take our time.
We have a lifetime of loving, after all.
Our work has given my skin a sheen,
I glow, bathed in dawnlight,
we are too busy to wait for the moon.
The hair on your belly calls
and rises in shivers.

I get big eyes, luminous,
enchanting to you.
Your big-body moves to cover me,
I welcome the weight with
sated purrs, your gruff response.
Whispers command and compel.
Move there, sweet, stop,
roll over, slowly baby.
Dazed, I comply,
lay still as I wait for the next step.
You watch us, pleasure me,
touching the soles of my feet,
behind my knees,
rubbing slow circles along my back,
whispering up my spine.
Helpless noises, soft, frantic mewlings ensue.
I feel your satisfaction, your smug.
You move your mouth and tongue
tracing diagrams on flesh.
Desperate, now I sidle closer,
your hand forces me down.
Be still, baby, still for me.
Quiescent, I comply,
you good girl, me
ramping rampantly
Still is so hard but the waiting,
soft commands,
thrill as I fight myself to obey.
I'm thinking, YES

I AM a good girl,
sexy chuckles at my struggle.
Trembling, hotter than I can remember being.
You....lap at me,
lips trailing heat as my body follows
touch.
You mouth me, sucking softly, pulling relentlessly
at things low within me.
I watch you, now,
willing you to bring that mouth back,
NOW!
I see your pink, wet tongue dart,
suddenly, tugging my nipple, licking tips to
urge a single droplet of sex sweat
to fall.
You tease it into your mouth, feeling it pucker.
Feels so good, wet, nasty sweet
I cry out,
close to screaming.
Your plunge into me
is a blessed relief.
You bring me.
I can't stop coming.
My last view is of you dipping a
thick finger into the wet
and clean your finger
like a cat....and
all goes dark.QUIESCENT

Aftermath.
So good, so sweet, so mine!
Exhaustion born of passion,
we lay curled,
basking at what we have done.
Musk shared replete,
awash in us.
My peanut butter thighs
shift restlessly,
amazingly wanting more.
I sense your movement and realize
that you are still hungry, too.
Furious, we laze now.
You touch me so delicately,
careful, yet determined.
I meet you with a kiss,
my body gives a green light,
and lover, you move!
Your big hands, rough fingers, gentle me,
but mutely demands more.
Sheets damp, we take our time.
We have a lifetime of loving, after all.
Our work has given my skin a sheen,
I glow, bathed in dawnlight,
we are too busy to wait for the moon.
The hair on your belly calls
and rises in shivers.
I get big eyes, luminous,
enchanting to you.

Your big-body moves to cover me,
I welcome the weight with
sated purrs, your gruff response.
Whispers command and compel.
Move there, sweet, stop,
roll over, slowly baby.
Dazed, I comply,
lay still as I wait for the next step.
You watch as pleasure me,
touching the soles of my feet,
behind my knees,
rubbing slow circles along my back,
whispering up my spine.
Helpless noises, soft, frantic mewlings ensue.
I feel your satisfaction, your smug.
You move, your mouth and tongue
tracing diagrams on flesh.
Desperate now, I sidle closer,
your hand forces me down.
Be still, baby, still for me.
Quiescent, I comply,
you good girl me,
ramping rampantly
Still is so hard but the waiting,
soft commands,
thrill as I fight myself to obey.
I'm thinking, YES
I AM a good girl,
sexy chuckles at my struggle.

Trembling, hotter than I can remember being.
You....lap at me,
lips trailing heat as my body follows
touch.
You mouth me, sucking softly, pulling relentlessly
at things low within me.
I watch you, now,
willing you to bring that mouth back,
NOW!
I see your pink, wet tongue dart,
suddenly, tugging my nipple, licking tips to
urge a single droplet of sex sweat
to fall.
You tease it into your mouth, feeling it pucker.
Feels so good wet nasty sweet
I cry out,
close to screaming.
Your plunge into me
is a blessed relief.
You bring me.
I can't stop coming.
My last view is of you dipping a
thick finger into the wet
and clean your finger
like a cat....and
all goes dark.

THE THREE OF US

Cedric Benson visited his high school best friend Rod to his penthouse one day. They have been together since they're at young age and in every little thing, they each shared. They grew up in that habits. Been a long time when they've seen each other because Rod and his family moved to another location but they didn't lose their communication as best friends. They spent the days and nights with lots of fun and adventurous weeks together. Until one day Rod's girlfriend visited him and a coincidence's, that his best friend's girlfriend was the girl in his dreams, "Thalia". Rod didn't know everything as he considered they both trusted each other

Cedric needed to go back home and Rod's car was not that big enough to store their things in, and Thalia was the last one to drop off.

"Ok," I said. "Then where is Thalia going to sit?"

I could see on his face he was trying to come up with a solution. "I got an idea," he said. He opened the passenger side door. He put his bag and files in the middle. He then got in and sat down. "See plenty of room". Here Thalia sat next to me." I tried to sit next to Cedric. I could sit in the seat, but the door wouldn't close. Now, I am not a big woman. I stand about five feet tall and I am weighing hundred pounds. It was Cedric taking up all the room. He was already over six feet tall and weighed around two hundred pounds. "It's not me that's taking up all of the room, it's you. This isn't going to work. Tell you what, leave your things back and when we come to visit you we'll bring it with us."

"No way," he answered as I got out of the car and stood by the door.

"Make up your mind, Rod, it's hot out here."

"Ok," Rod looked at me. "Ok, you can sit on my lap."

"Rod, it's five hours drive to your house," his best friend said.

"I know, but Thalia doesn't weigh much. What do you say, Thalia? Would you mind sitting on my lap?"

'Ok, I'll sit on your lap. But if it gets too uncomfortable I want to stop and rest" I said while looking at Rod, my boyfriend. He agreed. "Ok, let's get our lunch so we can get on the road."

We didn't take long. Since I would be sitting on Cedric's lap for five hours, I wanted to wear something really comfortable. My jeans would be too tight. Plus it was too hot to wear them. I looked in my closet. As I was going through my clothes I found a summer dress I bought. It was the short type with sleeveless arms. It buttoned up in front. I unbuttoned it and put it on. When I finished buttoning it up, I noticed it showed my bra too much. I took it off again. I removed my bra.

On the way back home, while we were traveling, and the car was moving, my whole body was rubbing Cedric's body and I can feel his breathing heavily while sniffing my hair.

A moment later, as Cedric placed his hands upon my lap,

'I can't bear these feeling Thalia,"

he whispered through my ears

His fingers bit by bit caressing my thighs which makes me grasps.

"would you mind if I placed my fingers inside?"

I was quite titillated by what he whispered and I can't control his desire. I opened up my two legs so he can freely feel and play my greedy clit...

" I love it, it feels good"

Thanks for massaging "

"Ohh really, lean on me so you'll feel better and relax" Cedric answered. "Honey! do what Cedric

says, still got a long way ride baby" my Boyfriend answered back on us. He cannot see us behind
Only my head and Cedric which half of my body covered him.

Along our way, Cedric begin to feel my body, his one hand was under my shirt playing my tits while the other hand underneath my panty, his fingers were wild and free in and out my wet pussy, I lifted a bit, unzipped his short and pulled his hard dick out, "ohh Thalia you're so gorgeous" I love what I am doing, as silently whispered and grasping,
"I wanna let my dick slide into you "
While on the road, the car was running, shaking, my boyfriend can't tell the difference.
Cedric was enjoying what he's doing as I sat down on his lap, I let him go deep and play inside my cunt like a soldier standing firm and rolling under the cave yard
As hot as hell we creampie I feel he had cum but he never stopped in that way "I still want to stay inside you, "ohh Thalia," I know you haven't cum and I want to fuck you one more time" and I want you to cum this time"
I looked at him and gave a sweet sweaty smile...
As Cedric wished, 1 hour left on the road, we both cum and reached the heavenly lust and luscious desires.

Without Rod knowing what Cedric and I did in the backseat of the car.

HE ASKED ONCE AGAIN...

Naughty girl in a playful mood
love that whispers purring
means eroticism is stirring
is that all you're wearing?
thoughts of erotic,
passionate sharing
so I could be sucking your tits
while you stroke me to see if it fits
is your flower wet and warm
anxious for an orgasm storm.
Wish I could see your thighs
very near your prize.
uuummnn
may I remove the towel
Y, will be my chosen vowel;
Snugness arouses me greatly

SULTRY SIPS

wanting your upper lips
taken in sultry sips
rock hard as your hand unzips
and grips the tip as we film an erotic clip
she takes off her silky slip
anxious for a milky trip
hoping his python doesn't rip
the tightness between her hip
slowly and sensually
into her pudding, he begins to dip.
remove the towel and
my python rises
she taunts and teases with
her sir prizes
anxious to squeeze his pipe
as she realizes
he goes deeper in kitty
than she recognizes
and once he cums,
it super-sizes
she takes it wetter and
wider than she advertises.
holding 8 inches in both hands;
he issues free flow cummands
wondering how much will squirt
no panties under her skirt!
tight wet and hot like shy's love

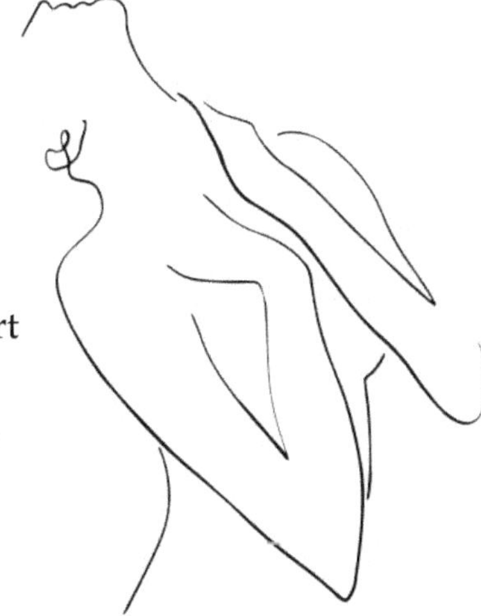

49

awesome sight watching
her tits bouncing above
full of chocolate pipe, then
suddenly his nutt oozes
all of shy's lips are ripe,
to taste the overflow she chooses.
I know your garden is wet
how deep could I get?
into your warm enter* net
when I explode will you be upset?
do you crave kissing this hot;
before he gives you a lot;
trying to hit that spot
giving you all he got;

MY PRINCE WISH

I would give you a bubble bath;
and massage you
with baby oil afterward.
have your dinner prepared.
then just let you, rest baby.
kissing your back
and legs while you sleep.
and if you are rested
and felt better,
maybe I could kiss you
in a few other places
until you showcased
that lovely smile.
I wish I was who you
came home to.
so I could invigorate your
favoured femininity.
obviously, you turned me on;
visual of your oral
with this milk bone;
teasing him to stretch
and deepen your silk zone;
then to kiss your erotic
lips as groan and moan,
couldn't leave chocolate
cocked alone.

SNUG'S PARADISE

She smiles knowing
how easily she does entice.
Thoughts of sperm flowing
into her snug paradise.
Inside of her, his pipe is growing and
she makes him cum twice.
Her erotic skills are showing
perky nipples taste so nice.
as he wonders about her thighs
squeezing his cock
and so he cannot pull out.
She cherishes the
length and size;
he has opened her wider
no doubt.
She is aggressive,
dick possessive,
and hot; the wettest
pussy he's ever come inside.
She sucked his dick a lot
and she agreed to ride.
He felt her release,
warmth did increase;
she moaned, whispered
"Your dick feels so good"
She climbed off to
suck his beast;

and swallowed his
cum like she should.
Her skin simply glowed
and shone; fulfilled with nutt,
she has never had so much.
He was kissing her curves
and body lines;
and she tingled with every touch.
He gazed at her moist kitty;
cum soaked and tired
from a relentlessly sensuous fucking.
He fingered her
and she looked so pretty;
and he began titty sucking.
She opened her sultry thighs;
and whispered,
"baby please fuck me rough again"
That "pleased"
looked in her eyes;
throbbing dick
was her best friend.

Smooth taunt thighs
accessing her to haunts guy
She loved the chocolate size
caused her skirt to rise
Erotic look in his eyes
to ride him might be wise.
Sensuous lust he hoped to disguise

cause she's freakier than orgasms advertise.

54

EJACULATION

Freeze blow losing pulse
lonely heart open mind
hurt me now and
let me feel the stiletto weapon
crushing stone
the pain I deserve yet I'm not weak
sitting in my face tasting your love
shackles bind strap you down
temptation oral thwack
your kitty sweet furry
white rosebud intoxicates desire
screwing hard play rough
sufficient pleasure
he ain't huge erect cock
erotica babe falls quietly
9 inches size I beg you, please
artful ways sin deep cum zealous
cover my flesh and together we
are orgasmic

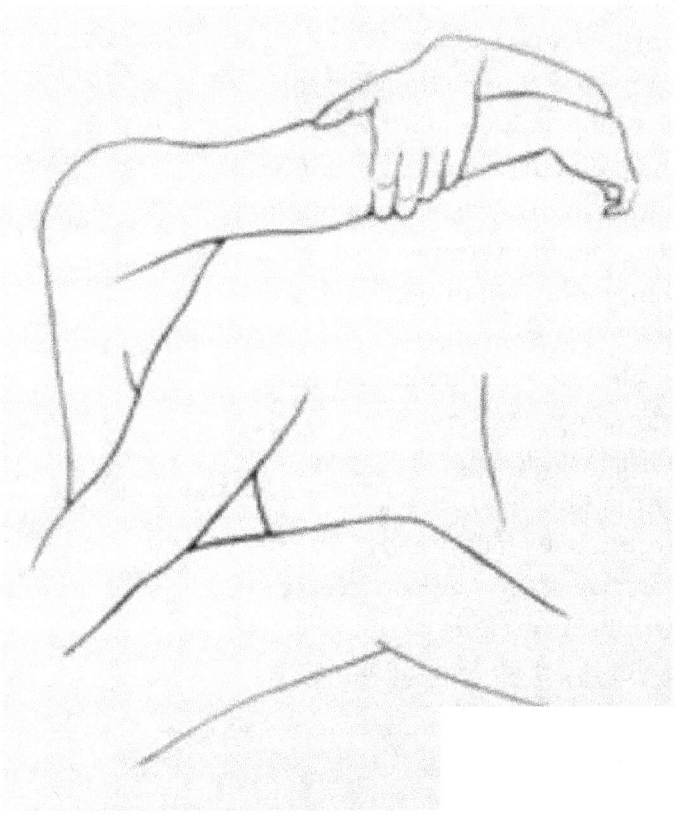

MOIST

Moist as she rubs her clit;
thoughts of long chocolate
bar hard large.
aroused sexy lady
makes his python fit
she loves the energetic charge.
hot and anxious to feel
his huge cock flood
her with Sperm
affectionately she does kneel;
knowing his dick
will make her squirm
luscious is her erotic appeal
she craves all pussitions.
so much a wild fuck can heal
to have chocolate soon
tingles her oasis nutritions

ALLURING GARDEN

Moist from coitus
and pussy well-eaten
she wants his amazing
dark cock.
Alluring garden
his cum will sweeten
saliva loosens
her kitty lock.
Horny as she
sucks him first
fondling and
licking his balls.
Aggressive blowjob
makes him burst
then enter her
vaginal walls.
Lady realizes
he is too thick
her wet entry
is tight and hot.
Kinky lady really
wants his huge
dick and she
knows, he'll cum a lot.
Unselfish as her thighs
spread wide she says
Baby, give me that

torpedo kinda slow
Heaven is tingling
wildly as she slides
inside, and her face
has that glow.

HUNGER OF THE DEAD

She knew his touch was death
Yet her lusts knew no fear
She reached out and laid hands upon him
Bringing to life the dormant bones
No flesh enhanced him
No feelings of love
Or lust or desire or life
Just hunger.

She knew his touch was death
Yet her hands sought him
Caressed into life his repressed need
She breathed her fire into him
His soul stood ready
Her kisses inflamed
His hunger.

She knew his touch was death
Yet life was her eternal gift
Her hands, her lips raised his spirit
Erect and alive he danced
Power ignited within
Tension mounted
With hunger.

She knew his touch was death
Yet she opened her body

He entered finally erect and on fire
His burning member-owned her
Orgasm possessed her
Ejaculation too soon
Hunger abated

CHOCOLATE GUY

Beautiful sultry princess
claims to be shy
but loves a 9 inches
chocolate guy.
Lips aroused as they
refuse to pass by
the throbbing cock
she's anxious to try.
Accept it she does
and kinda feeling high
it's like a drug to slurp
a thickness she cannot deny.
Cumpelling throat
was asking why
but now her tongue
will palate is no longer dry.
Kreme drips from her lips
to each thigh kitty so hott
all she can do is sigh.
Creamy nuggat some
got in her eye
she uses her tongue
to wipe cum with no alibi.
Oasis orgasms
mandingo cannot deny
python headed toward
her Cheery Cherry pie.

Confessing and confirming
a chocolate fetish
she cannot deny
slurpee suds she swallows,
oh.. my! my! my!
Kinky freaky tight kitty
her tingle did not lie
waiting so long
for her Adonis and she asks,
."Why?"

63

HIS WET DREAMS

He was about to sleep last night
suddenly, he messaged me saying "goodnight"
I responded with lots of kisses and hugs
"goodnight baby, have a rest and sleep tight"
He then falls asleep
after we talked, he whispered:
"I want you tonight lying on my bed"
and he kissed me some more
before switching off his phone
"I love you, baby,
wishing you're here tonight"
He feels me with his teasing tongue
he let his feelings and desire spelt out of my milky
complexion as he coitus deeper and deeper he
exploited and cum
in his witty dream, I don't want him to stop
I beg and said
 "I want more and more until the morning light"
He loves the things I did in his dream
Slept in his chest, caresses his lips
 his sweats, scattered all over my hips
as he plunged deeper and deeper inside my tight
pink-pussy cat
With every thirst, we filled our lusts
as our souls played romantically the game of love
giving him pleasure even if its a dream

giving him satisfaction, dreaming about me making love every now and then.

YOUR PRETTY LIPS

He did taste my
nectar with each word;
and orgasm has occurred.
As he's giving me erotic head;
while I was his prose and;
I believed I'm in his bed.
Scanning each verse
it's like I just came
and he rode me and
kept moaning my name
"I love what you do,
you're my lover,
I would select,"
 I whispered while teasing his lips.

"Make me squirt
all over your pretty lips;
I want your tongue
ready as the python unzips,
Baby, you're sexy
with those sultry nipples ripe;
I wish we could do doggy-style
as u tried to type.
Make me harder
and harder before
I push it deep;
and every warm drop

I want you to keep.

HER NAKEDNESS

the erection she enticed
and the length she caused
he can only imagine
the aggressiveness
of making love to her;
and the overflowing lustrous release.
Her skin complexions, awesome
and that snug kitty
looks scrumptious
and of course
the most enchanting thighs

CUM CAN BE VERB OR NOUN

Even better in you
love the way you tease
the towel was very Erotic
I love the way you tease
the towel was very erotic
it makes me horny so please
let me enter your garden
and water your beautiful flower
would 9 inches make
you cum and scream
you inhabit my
naughtiest dream
behind that towel is
a snug kitty anxious
for dark cock
you do realize I'm
hard as a rock
if I lay my cock over your shoulder
will your mouth become my dick holder
love those thighs
I want them to wrap around
to see the look in your eyes,
enjoying 9 inches of brown
dick dang near drags the ground
 sliding deep is an awesome wet sound
lovely and sexy woman I've found,
cum can be a verb and a noun.

TOUCH ME JUST LIKE THAT

A night to remember
A savage kiss from you, stranger
masculine body touches my skin.

Your desire and mine arouses our souls
alluring caress of finger to the whole
come, feel, and tease my milky skin
with your Harding throbbing vein.

Rhythms of our body language
dancing, beyond romantic moonlit
your touch, kiss, and flaming tongue,
rolling around my pinkish tits.

As I waited, to your sweet nectar
your whisper, killing me softly
breathless as I moan g
with your strokes and deep coitus.

Cum as I cum all through the night
your erection makes me witty,& wild
don't stop giving such pleasure
for us strangers, as we feed our naked souls.

DELIGHTFUL TIME

Time to imagine the wonderful world of fantasy
I love to swim and lurk around your broad chest
TO feel your muscles in between your legs
TO guide your erecting vein into my hunger cave
And let your flowing sweaty spread through my
lusting clit
What a wonderful night and time of illusion that
makes me feel greedy
this flirty moment while it's you that I think

BREATHLESS

I
want
to feel
your gentle
touch and sweet
Wiesenthal runs through
my milky skin your whisper that
makes me gasp and moan while your fingers
streaming my long
blonde hair... I miss to
hold and rub your
throbbing vein
Mostly when
you tease
my tits
that
makes me feel misbehaving

DREAMERS DREAM

I was thinking about you last night
while lying down, staring my dim light
hallucinating, you were at my side
teasing caressing me so tender so wild.
My illusions began, setting fire and flame
eternal flames that burn my soul
the heat from your masculinity form
that tickles my inner sensation
showering with your love and tender kisses
through my milky complexion, and I laid back
sigh deep grasps like no air to breathe in and out
pulling off my flimsy sleeping gown
and slowly, cuddled me and let me lie down.
I can't find myself while your fingers, running
all over my face and your teasing tongue, playing
my pinky tiny tits
And am out of control, my hips that bumped up
and down dancing through the rhythm of your
silent musical instrument undying moaned
in my four-sided square room you and me
against the fire of eternal flames
A hilarious throbbing vein entered my private cave
and begun to be wild hard and firm
my luscious moment absurd heavenly desired
submerged our fleshes flowed hottest moves
moved so calmed feels good cause it warmed
deep inside my witty cave, you're the master

key that opened my lonely caved.
We both cum, and never go down
As I loved to feel you moving, asking more time
dreamers dream sexy, wet hot, and wild
I woke up, touching my tits playing my cave
fingers placed through my clit.

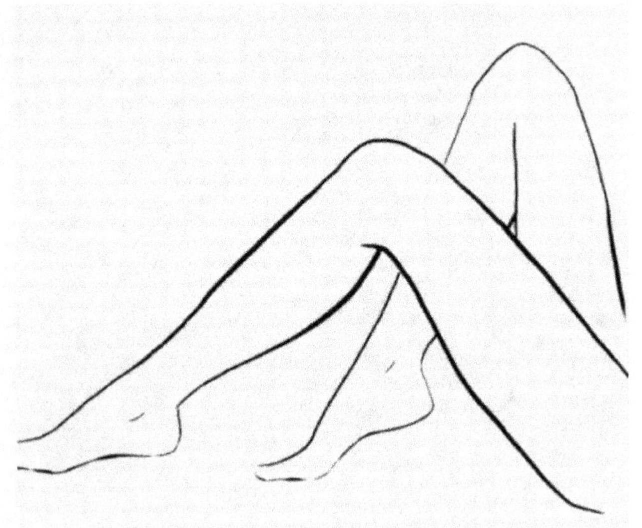

NUMEROUS ON THE WALL

When I heard him moaned
and holding me tighter
than the beginning
while he looks at me
and his eyes start begging...
I feel the sensual pleasure
and satisfaction
of what he'd been doing
I love those sweet and
tender caresses
his desires in the name of love
his unique passion for romance
I feel the hot libido inside
I feel the hardest part
of his manhood
as he comes aggressive,
I can't hold my breath no more
And we become more glamorous
than ever, until the fire of
eternal flame comes to an end

ONE LONELY NIGHT

One lonely night
I found a knight
He asked for a drink
I gave my white ink.

I was worried
And, I was weird
My ink did drip
Into his lips.

Was it a sane
Or just a game
Of a thirsty throat
Of a knight in the porch

JUST YOU AND I

I saw your manhood fitted and firm
the way you wore your wet looks
I've been dreaming of that sweet caress
those gentle kisses to my longing lips

I have waited for you for so long
to feel this awesome feeling
'never expect that you'll step into my life
and here we are, we became one and united

Your milky complexion that turns the heat
Your gentle touch around my neck
those savage kisses between my legs
feels so good, it makes me moaned and grasped

I love the way you hold my back
ticklish, and your luscious touch
can this feeling will never end
I want you, need you, every now and then.

Just You and I
in this romantic room
let's fill out of love and passion
Just you and I, you and I.

MAGNOLIA

The memory beyond your tree
while resting with the couples of bee
your scenes that's sweet- intoxicating
petals that are lovely, passionate attractions.

I love to pick and taste your pollen grain
can't help to urge as I gazed through
your pinkish feminish reflection
desire with intimate affection.

Magnolia, you're a seductive flower
I can't control myself to quiver
I long to suck your sweet nectar
to absurd my thrust and thirsty condition.

As wild as my imagination
your flirty looks that are full of passion
igniting lust through compassion
with my greedy sensual momentum.

PRICK

He moves with his pumping vein,
I am begging to be touched
with his sly fancy eyeing
I feel his ironic muscle
and I begin to feel flame
Thighs shift,
placing in a comfortable
lovely steady position.
world of silence where the room
darkened with window blinds
his fingers slide and slip
away into a milky complexion
of my nakedness
Tongue freely tastes my skin
arousing breathes,
I sigh, I gasp! I moan!
You stop suddenly...
I guide your fingers to my loin
down to the opening,
hands unclenched
no fear, your fingers
stroking my pussy!
it feels-good inside out
I wait for your throbbing
and harding vein
to prick my virginity
and oh!!! pain

suddenly endured
you're so gentle even
when you coitus
hard and deep

AND THE MOON SHARED THE LIGHT

And the moon shared the light
entire the universe
and my darkened room,
like a dim light begins to glow
like the blinking light
that brighten up the disco pub
and from far beyond,
I saw your shadow,
dancing in rhythm
of the blowing wind.
Far, across the pool
of the dancing hall,
I made a move and walk
towards you.
you heard my steps
and looked at me suspiciously
so turned around and
face-to-faced, you stood up and asked me;
"What do you want from me?"
I was tensed when you asked and suddenly, I felt
like I'm frozen.
I mumbled and you did hear
what I've said, you smiled
so sweet, you hold my hands up
and you asked me to dance
in the dancing hall, I was

shocked by then, I talked to you softly
while we were dancing
"I'm not a man, nor a woman,
I'm a bisexual human being" and
lowered my head cause I can't fight
the feeling that I felt for you.
"Rejection! Yeah, damned word rejection!
was the word I truly hate to hear from
the one I admired"
Yet, instead of pushing me away from you,
you pulled me out from the crowd and
you whispered through my ears
"I don't care about who you are!
all I know is I like you like what you mumbled a
while ago", and you smiled at me
again, I saw those two dimples saying
"Love me as you do"
And we went furthermore
We ended up in a hotel room
The aggressiveness was there
like you seemed to be so familiar
with my body curves and crevice.
You knew where to find the place
you want to touch. I let you feel
every detail of my body, and I can't
stop you from caressing my skin. Your fingers
lingered in, ironically. I end up grasping.
your mouth hunting my mouth

and I let your tongue play around, sucking in and
up while your other hand is busy playing my
cunt..."ohhh heaven's sake!
I have never felt this way; until you came and let
me know how
luscious feelings of having you.
Your tongue is better
than a man's erect cock
Your fingers that were free to feel deeply
as you came in and out,
while your tongue sucking my clit
We foreplay the first time being oneness
I was your student at that time.
I feel your breasts suck my tits,
licks my flimsy skin and tease my clit,
As you curved my back I went through
your juicy cunt, slides my hand and let my two
fingers in your cunt
sweet nectar I have tasted
while you enjoyed the way I aroused your
titillating facial expression
you pulled me up
And kissed me, sucked my tongue again and again.
I licked your back ears and whispered
"let's cum together I can't hold myself no more"
As we were both bisexual,
we kissed each other, our clits cling together
while our hands massaged each breast
until orgasmic came and cum together

that sweet and romantic night
the first time I made love to a
Sweet girlfriend where I found my
happiness and satisfaction

This was not the first and last yet
It's just the beginning of my second
time falling in love.

HI,

my name is Celina,
and I am your woman for tonight
I will be your private love so please,
turn off the light
I'll be your mysterious lover
your masculinity arouses me.
let your eight inches long
dark chocolate melt into my mouth
ummm I love the taste
your dripping syrup!
I want to lick every single drop of it.
this romantic silent night,
you will moan and grasp!
and this lonely bedroom,
will bring you joy,
These luscious lips that full of desire,
will lead the way to your heart
your forbidden darkened room
every twilight time of yours, hunger strike
I'll give you the lustrous flirting
game
that you ever missed since then
just one thing for sure
be gentle with my thighs,
I am a lady, without experience
at the age of eighteen
I choose you to be the first

one who will rip off my heart
my chosen one, who I secretly
admired and loved

BUSINESS APPOINTMENT

I took a Business Trip out of town, I'm a naughty
girl so I'm going to play around.
I caught the eye of the CEO, and they caught my
eye at first sight...
I was invited to a private dinner and drinks, they
smiled and gave me a devilish wink.
Dinner was delicious and erotically sublime, so I
allowed them to cross the professional line.
I was given the key to their hotel suite, so we could
get to know each other and properly meet.
I let myself into the dim-lit room, my heart started
pounding going boom...boom...
boom
There were Rose petals on the carpeted floor,
leading to the opened bedroom door.
The shower was running and the room was full of
steam, I felt myself starting to glisten and gleam.
As they stepped out of the bath I collapsed to my
knees, they whispered one word and that word
was PLEASE.
SHE wanted me to eat her inside and out, nope it
wasn't a male like you originally thought.
Being that I was hungry and thirsty for some
flavorful Cunt, all she could do was just lay there
and shriek, pant, and grunt.

Here comes the white trickle streaming down her legs, I made sure my freakish appetite was satisfyingly fed.

FEEL ME

The rain has come to end,
unfinished lavish ripping soul
yearning another pouring rain
to fulfill an intimate moment.

Fancying the puddles around
while lurking in and out
twirling all over the floor
spinning merry-go-round.

Feel me within your touch
caress oh, thy flimsy skin
strum that long silky hair
undress me with your tongue.

Your titillating, passionate moves
your seductive whispers in my ear
your heart that beats unpredictable
your urging deck so tough and firm.

Feel the senses of my presence
and let your muscle runs through my cave
like a toddler that sucks when hunger strikes
serve delightfully, your throbbing vein
with this witty cave again and again

STRANGERS IN PARADISE

I long for an eternal love
that will fade my lust
satisfy my addiction
hungry for your touch.

Come closer to me
feel my heartbeats
don't be afraid, wanna play
unwrap my guilty pleasure.

Embrace me, undress me
just become my desire
I'm fueled by that gaze
stranger, how I count the ways.

Ahhh, your breath, whispers in my ear
sweet poetry that grips me
running fingers across my breast
tender caressing, cheek blushing.

I try to hold you back the urge
to moan and moan again
driven by a luscious desire
your tongue that circles to my stiff nipples.

You pulled me up, Ohh dancing lips
pushed you down onto my bed

serving delight what a pleasure!
I love the stroke of your sacred flame.

TOWEL'S TRICK(ACROS-EROTIC)

Tender: as she lathers each place where a rigid
python would love to probe.
Oasis: the allure of her pretty face, ummnn allow
me to dis-robe.
Wants: to feel a man of steel, consistent passionate
thrusts into her Love Cave.
Erotic: is how she needs to feel, she is excited to be
cum an orgasm slave.
Loving: that she truly needs, aroused by those
thick, long chocolate inches.
ripe for a burst of sperm seeds, oh how her ecstasy
urges his wet python quenches.
WHITE BUSH OF ROSE

You reclined within heaven
between my thighs and legs.
Sentients my white has sensed
a deft decision-maker I chose you.
Faith, knowing, lead your arrow
straight lush is a state of mind
cracking the coated candy core
your scents so sweet.
revel, roll, crawl gritting teeth
as sugar engulfed frenzy minded,
all out of control bound fast,
blind and bound is pleasing,
swift action, delightful!

tongue rasping over inner ear,
whispers promising
wet and lurid he licks.
riding me down with pleasures '
road, he grips, wringing
hollers no one should ever hear
nut sweeting, he knows
when it's really so come,
have it drift in dreams,
awaken, screaming
more, more more!!!
hesitance improbable
resistance impossible
a pantheon of old, forgotten gods
praise our inevitable fall,
into the deep, blushed lush
of the white bush of rose...

BAR IN THE CORNER

That bar in the corner
where I brought you
to hardness
beneath the table
while I flirted with you
never once missing a stroke,
your mischievous looks
and eyes knowing all.
That bedroom
in Crete where
I grasped your hips
as though I was drowning,
pulling you on to me,
the ferocity of lust
leaving us breathless,
impaled on each other's heat,
your calloused hands
feeling the sweat
the slickness of my breasts
as I leaned back
into your neck
and you murmured
beautiful filth...
The nights we loudly
burned right through
all the safe words
singularly intent

on devouring the flesh,
the meat, the sweetness
of our human selves,
spinning out in to
the carnal dark
begging for release,
begging for the denial
of release, begging for more,
more
"ahh!!! I want you more!"
my lips on your lips
finding the sweet spot
that made you arch your body,
making the most beautiful bridge
as you came to
the first shuddering,
skin raking,
hair pulling rising and release.
Those days when the
shoreline and the sea
were forever intimates
endlessly fascinated
by the mirror shape of the other,
continuously exploring,
continuously finding
the familiar new,
looking to each other
with tenderness.

LOVE AND LUST DELIRIOUSLY PAID

when the person you loved,
deliriously excited to have
sex with you after all.
and he has nothing to call
he'll whisper to the wind
your sweet intense name...
"Celine! oohh my Celine"!
you are so lovely my queen!
with your lustrous beauty;
I beg you to stay! stay with me...
those whispers, run out to your
nerves, through your vein,
ohh my Celine my beauty queen!
your beauty displayed,
and never been betrayed
like succulent lemonade
view,.. sip,....and...tingled...
please don't fade
you're the best in the shade;
I lusted for the love you gave
and what we had made;
passion's the perkiest upgrade;
ecstasy foundation laid
orgasm dues well paid;

ABOUT THE AUTHOR

BELEN RAPADA ESPOSO (a.k.a. Shy Lhen Esposo) is an Overseas Filipino Worker in Singapore. Born on November 22, 1975 in Barangay San Antonio Cabangan Zambales Philippines.

She is a single mother of three namely: Rhica Marie,(23) Mary Jane,(22), and Ken Cirnel (19) while Joyce (22) and Jessa(21)are her two foster children. Belen Esposo has studied and finished the courses

Nursing Aide Caregiver babysitting and elderly care in 2011, Basic Aromatherapy in 2012, Basic Cosmetology in 2013, Taekwondo 2014, Advance Baking 2017 Basic Guitar Lesson (unfinished) in FOWS (Filipino Overseas Workers of Singapore) at Bayanihan Centre, Pasir Panjang Rd. Singapore.

Belen or Shy Lhen Esposo is a self-published author of

"Shy I Love You Today and Tomorrow", published on April 24, 2019 "Dreams Are My Reality" was published on September 26, 2019, and "Shy Hawk's Path" Published in February 2020.

She is also an author contributor of "Get Lucky" book an anthology book of Philippine and Singapore Writings published in 2015 by Ethos Book. She joined the poetry festival workshop in July 2016 and became a featured poet on May 20, 2017 (Regardless of Race)and January 7, 2018. A 3RD Runner Up winner of NUCLEUS POEM MOTHER LANGUAGE DAY on February 18, 2018, and joined the

 Get Lucky an anthology book of Philippine and Singapore Writings event on February 18, 2019, that also marks the opening of Filipino Costumes Across Islands and Eras: A Photography Exhibit, curated by the University of the Philippines Alumni Association in Singapore (UPAAS), the exhibit showcases traditional Filipino costumes(Maria Clara) across the three main island groups of Luzon, Visayas, and Mindanao. Through a series of photographs, the exhibit will also demonstrate how the more popular costumes have evolved with time and how, despite the many variants, there is always a binding element that unifies the colors and fabrics into a distinct Filipino aesthetic.

A 3RD RUNNER UP POET MIGRANT WRITERS COMPETITION on November 10, 2019. Shy Lhen is also a poet contributor at NOMAD'S CHOIR POETRY JOURNAL at Woodside New York, New York. She also collaborated with Nick Ambrister *THE POETRY OF SHY LHEN ESPOSO AND NICK AMBRISTER

THE ACE SERIES about the German pilot who fell in love with Shy the Jewish lady. And THROUGH OPEN HANGAR DOOR which covers the love and space traveling a trip to the stars, and was published.

Being a foreign domestic worker, was not easy for Shy Lhen to be far and away from her loved ones. So to relieve homesickness, she managed to encourage herself to find a way to escape sadness, and she ended up writing. And to think about her children's future. This passion for arts in writing inspired her and to develop and learn something new about her daily life living. Her passion for writing didn't end up in poetry, she is also a lyricist, her first song lyrics titled "AFRAID TO DIE" had been released last June 2020 with the help of Migrant Workers of Singapore (MWS) through the help of the Migrant Band the DAB (Dreams Arrived Band) from Bangladesh. Instead of sobbing in the corner, and a plain domestic helper, she ends up being a Filipino Migrant Poet Writer Novelist, and Song lyricist. As she captured the beautiful meaning of life.

www.ingramcontent.com/pod-product-compliance
Lightning Source LLC
LaVergne TN
LVHW020911200726
843506LV00011B/1669